Bumper and Noah

Bumper and Noah

Mary Hollingsworth

Illustrated by Rick Incrocci

Chariot Books™
A Division of Cook Communications

Special Thanks

To Tom Moore,
a creative and talented friend,
who helped give Bumper
his personality.

Scripture quoted from *New Century Version*., copyright © 1991 by Word Publishing, Dallas, Texas 75039. Used by permission.

Scripture verses marked (TLB) are taken from *The Living Bible* © 1971. Used by permission of Tyndale House Publishers, Inc., Wheaton, IL 60189. All rights reserved.

Look at the behemoth.
    I made him just as I made you.
    He eats grass like an ox.

Look at the strength he has in his body.
    The muscles of his stomach are powerful!

His tail extends like a cedar tree.
    The muscles of his thighs are woven together
.

His bones are like tubes of bronze metal.
    His legs are like bars of iron.

He is one of the first of God's works.

Job 40:15 19a
Holy Bible, New Century Version

The Bible doesn't say much about dinosaurs. It doesn't say how Noah gathered all the animals onto the Ark, either. Use your imagination and pretend. Maybe, just maybe, it happened like this...

Bumper the dinosaur leaned against a fig tree, eating a tasty fig. He sat very, very still.

Now, sitting still was not easy for Bumper. Bumping things with his huge tail and big flat feet was much easier. But Bumper had decided that today he would not bump anything. He would just sit very still.

Soon Bumper said, "I am thirsty. I will be very careful and not bump anything when I move. But I must have a drink of water."

Bumper splashed into the brook for a drink and bumped the beavers' dam, crushing it flat. Quickly he backed up, bumping into a whole family of opossums hanging from their favorite tree branch. "Clumsy Bumper!" Mrs. Opossum yelled. "Stay away from my tree!"

He turned to run away and stepped on a sleeping lion's tail. The lion woke with a ROAR! A frightened Bumper spun around. BOOM! His big tail knocked the bees' honeycomb down. Angry bees buzzed everywhere. "Why do you always have to bump, you clumsy Bumper?" asked one angry bee, stinging Bumper on his tender nose. Ouch!

Bumper ran through the forest bumping trees and rocks and animals. "It's just like Great-grandpa Bumper used to say. We Bumpers bump into things. It's always been that way." Bumper sighed sadly. "I come from a long line of Bumpers."

He'd heard the story since he was just a little fellow. Bumper's great, great, great, great, great, great Grandfather Bumper was the first dinosaur way back there in the Garden of Eden.

While Bumper was still thinking, a beautiful white dove landed on a branch above him.

"Hello, Bumper," she said. "My name is Whisper. I have an urgent message for you."

"Me? Are you sure you have the right dinosaur?"

"Yes, I am quite sure," she said. "You need to go to Noah's giant boat as fast as you can." (Everyone in the forest had heard about Noah's giant boat.) "He has a special job that only you can do."

"Yes, of course!" said Bumper, jumping up, accidentally bumping his tail against Whisper's tree. "Sorry," he said as the dove fluttered out of the way.

"Wait!" called Bumper. "How do I find Noah's boat?"

"Easy," said Whisper. "Go to Fig Tree Valley over the big hills." She pointed to the south with her wing.

"What will I do when I get there?" asked Bumper

"Noah will show you," Whisper answered.

Bumper looked up at the big hills in the distance.
"Good-bye, Whisper, and thanks!"

He ran toward the hills as fast as he could go, bumping into
rocks and trees along the way. As he ran, he sang, "Noah
needs me, Noah needs me. Clumsy old Bumper.
Noah needs me!"

Suddenly he stopped. His feet wouldn't move. Worse than
that, he was sinking. Quicksand! The harder he tried to
push and pull himself out, the deeper he sank.

"Don't worry, Bumper. I'll help you!" an elephant trumpeted.
Bumper grabbed the elephant's trunk with his front legs. *Swoosh!*
Plop! Bumper landed on dry ground.

"Thanks," Bumper said. "I'm on my way to help Noah.
He *needs* me."

After that, Bumper paid attention to where he ran. At last he had to stop to rest. He lay down on a patch of soft green grass and fell fast asleep.

When Bumper woke up, he couldn't see the big hills. The sky had turned cloudy and gray. He didn't know what to do! How would he find Noah's boat? Bumper sat very, *very* still for the first time in his life.

Finally, a playful wind sent by God chased the clouds away, and Bumper saw the big hills again. Laughing, Bumper bumped an apple tree and caught the falling apples for his lunch.

Slowly Bumper trudged over the big hills, singing "Noah needs me, Noah needs me. Clumsy old Bumper. Noah needs me!"

As he entered beautiful Fig Tree Valley, he saw Noah building the giant boat.

"Just in time," Noah called to Bumper. "I have a special job for you. You can use your tail to help bump these boards into place."

Bumper nodded happily, glad to see Noah and ready to help him any way he could.

Bumper and Noah's family worked hard to finish
building the giant boat. It felt good to help.

"It's done," Noah said, looking up at Bumper. "Thank you for helping us. Now I have a surprise for you. God has chosen you to live on this boat with us when the big rains come. Welcome aboard!"

Suddenly bird songs filled the air and the ground began shaking with the sound of tramping feet. Animals of every kind came from the forest and meadows, up over the big hills, and down into Fig Tree Valley.

Bumper couldn't believe his eyes! He'd never seen so many animals. Best of all, bumping along in the crowd was Betsy, the prettiest girl dinosaur he'd ever seen. He ran to meet her, and together they bumped their way onto the giant boat.

Then, after all the animals climbed and flew and crawled onto the giant boat, Bumper started to bump the door closed. But before he could touch it, God closed the door for them. At the very same time, it started to rain.

For the next forty days, the rain came down. Inside the giant boat, Bumper and all the animals and Noah's family stayed dry.

Early one morning when Bumper woke up, he noticed something different. He gently bumped Betsy. "Wake up!" he whispered. "Listen."

"Listen to what? I don't hear anything."

"That's what I mean. IT'S STOPPED RAINING!" Bumper didn't mean to yell, but he couldn't help himself. He woke everyone up, but today they didn't care.

Bumper hoped he could run and play on dry ground right away. Instead, it took months for the water to dry up.

Finally, all the animals came off the boat to a clean new world. Two by two they set off to find themselves new homes. Bumper and Betsy hoped to find a brook and a fig tree to live near.

Bumper turned and looked back at Noah to wave good-bye. He was glad his bumping had helped Noah.

God has given each of you some special abilities; be sure to use them to help each other.

I Peter 4:10a (TLB)

You can read the story of Noah and the Ark in your Bible: Genesis 6—9.

DinoFacts

• What happened to the dinosaurs? The earth and its environment were different after the Flood. Maybe the dinosaurs couldn't survive as well in the new world. Maybe people killed some of them. God hasn't told us just when they became extinct, or died out. They lived for some time after the Flood, but we don't know just how long. Many animals besides dinosaurs have become extinct.

• Where did dinosaurs come from? God created them! He created all animals. See Genesis 1:20-25.

• Are dinosaurs in the Bible? Yes, but the Bible calls them by other names, like *behemoth* and *tannin*. Read Job 40:15-19.

• Were dinosaurs on the ark? The Bible says Noah should bring two of every living animal on the ark, so yes, dinosaurs must have been included. See Genesis 6:19, 20.

• What were the dinosaurs like? They probably were not killers. They ate mostly green plants and fruits.